About the Author

Terry Sewell is a very new writer on the scene. He writes from the heart, with an imagination that takes the reader to a place of beautiful fantasy and dreams. Terry has had ambitions of writing stories that everybody wants to read since his early childhood.

Dedication

I dedicate this story to all the people who believe in me, especially Sue, my loving wife, along with my deceased father, who always said... I was useless! Thank you to my publishers for giving me the chance to prove him wrong. Finally, for anyone who purchases a copy, I hope you enjoy it as much as I enjoyed writing it. Thank you.

Terry Sewell

THE BATTLE OF THE REDS AND THE GREYS

AUSTIN MACAULEY
PUBLISHERS LTD.

A CIP catalogue record for this title is available from the British Library.

ISBN 9781785542923 (Paperback)
ISBN 9781785542930 (Hardback)
ISBN 9781785542947 (E-Book)

www.austinmacauley.com

First Published (2016)
Austin Macauley Publishers Ltd.
25 Canada Square
Canary Wharf
London
E14 5LQ

Chapter One

Furry awoke late and found she was alone, although she could clearly hear the sound of her family and friends in the distance. The tireless squirrels out on an early morning raid for food were quite boisterous as they scampered around the leaf covered woodland bed, close to Hollow Trunk, the place they called home.

The red squirrel, just days old, gave a big stretch followed by a quick yawn, and moved off hurriedly to join the others. In the excitement she slipped on a wet twig and lost her balance, cracking her head on a metal object sticking out of the ground.

"Ouch, that hurt!" the tiny bushy tailed youngster cried out. She had a fresh cut and a dazed expression on her face.

Angel, her mother, was instantly at her side, having seen her overenthusiastic loved one topple over.

"There now," Angel said, repeatedly licking the bleeding wound. "You must be more careful young lady and a lot wiser before you start to hunt with us, now then!"

Sherman, Furry's father, then joined them. He smiled at his daughter's little calamity and laughed to warn her, "You'll learn," then moved off back to join the rest of the party, who were still busy collecting vital supplies for winter.

Chapter Two

The day quickly turned into night; Furry listened to the owls calling each other from deep within the forest's core. She could clearly hear the magical sound of the otters taking a midnight swim in the nearby creek. The moon was full and the stars were out. Furry and most of the creatures in the woods snuggled down and slept.

Slugger addressed a group meeting the next day, having heard news from the warren that the greys were on the move, reportedly threatening to wipe out the red community.

The old but wise leader of the reds dismissed all claims, playing down any reports as just hearsay. He told them all to go about their duties as normal. Secretly, however, he gathered a search party out into the notorious dark side, the home of the greys, in the hope of finding out what they were up to.

There was an air of tension surrounding the normally relaxed, happy haven of Forest Bright Side. The day had begun in full sunshine, with the sun's rays beautifully high-lighting a mass of snowdrops around Hollow Trunk. Dark clouds were forming on the horizon now though.

Furry ventured outside for the first time of the day.

"Don't go far now child," Angel warned her.

Chapter Three

Furry felt full from her breakfast as she sat, contented, watching the young rabbits from the warren frolicking about in the sunshine. They danced around and around in the leaves and looked so happy, having a really wonderful time.

Then out of the blue came a gunshot!

Lord Grief was on the rampage with a pheasant shoot!

The whole of the forest life took cover from the gentry invaders. The gun had terrified the life out of all the inhabitants within the vicinity. Angel quickly rescued

Furry, lifting her by the mane with her teeth into the safety of Hollow Trunk. The pair sat shaking in fear for their lives. Humans lined the width of the woodland, banging sticks while shouting, seeking out all potential fowl for shooting in the forest land.

It seemed to go on forever, yet it ended as quickly as it had started, leaving an atmosphere of complete silence. In the aftermath of it all everyone in Bright Side was left in shock. They stopped and took time to venture out and survey the scene. The smell of the gun smoke slowly disappeared; the muffled laughter of Lord Grief and his shooting party drifted out of earshot.

Chapter Four

That night Slugger and his brave recruits slipped quietly away while everyone was asleep under the stars. They hoped to arrive on the Dark Side, the home of the grey squirrels, before first light. It was a long, treacherous journey through a territory of unknown hidden dangers.

They were lucky to have Slugger's vast experience and knowledge of the gigantic forest land to guide them to the greys' borders.

They arrived earlier than they had anticipated, so they took a deserved drink and rest by Grey Brook before setting off boldly to enter the feared hostility within the greys' camp.

As dawn broke out on the dark side, a storm was brewing in the distance. The air was quite humid with bad light all around. Sherman, Slugger's bodyguard, was the first to rise from their short rest.

"Come on men," he whispered. "Let us take up our positions."

Quietly they surrounded the camp and lay in wait until Slugger gave the order to go in. There seemed a strange silence around the greys' territory, and it didn't take Slugger long to realise that something was not quite right.

As suspected, having given the signal to move in, things were definitely amiss. The place was totally deserted; not a grey squirrel in sight. Slugger nestled his head in his paws and feared the worst.

Chapter Five

A young rabbit scout who had ventured out of the warren to see what all the commotion was about, confirmed Slugger's suspicions. The greys had moved out days ago! Slugger's arch rival Barkeye had obviously out-thought him.

In despair, he could only hope and pray for all their families and friends back on Bright Side. The sounds of lightning and thunder broke out all around them as they hastily made their retreat from the Dark Side towards home.

When they arrived back, it was obviously clear they were too late. The greys had already raided their homes with many casualties, some of which were fatal. Sherman was gutted and felt both sick and angry at the same time, having realised that his family had been taken as hostages.

The weather took a change for the better as the demoralised group sat in mourning for the loss of their friends and family members.

Slugger paused to try and think of a plan of action to rescue the survivors of his beloved race.

Angel had been taken prisoner in an old disused log camp left by the humans, which the greys had now made into a temporary refuge. She had put up such a fight to save her youngster Furry from any harm, but there were too many of them. She now lay badly injured with Furry alongside, licking her wounds.

Chapter Six

Barkeye and his beloved Lady Grey entered the wooden cell that Angel and Furry were being kept captive in.

"Where's your leader now, hey! Nowhere, that's where," he chuckled to himself while prodding Angel's gaping wound with his paw.

"Leave her alone, you big brute!" Furry squealed out, while trying to pull his paw away from her mother's injury.

But he was just too strong. With one clean sweep from his paw he simply brushed her aside; "Get out of my way you sniffling half breed. By the time I have finished with your lot, you'll be wiped out forever. Then at last both kingdoms will be mine!"

"Yes, that is so right, the mighty greys will reign supreme!" Lady Grey butted in.

"Shut up woman! We can't stand here wasting time talking to this rabble. Let's just leave them to rot."

As the cell door opened, Furry instinctively made a dart for it. With her mother dying she knew there was only one hope left – to take a chance on finding help.

Barkeye was somewhat taken aback by the speed of the youngster's escape.

"Let her go, she won't get far!" he said with another chuckle.

Furry ran as fast as she could go with several greys in chase until she could run no further. She dropped down in her tracks to the forest floor. Luckily, she had fallen in front of a friendly fox's lair…

Chapter Seven

Sunlight, the friendly fox, heard the thud outside her hidden home. She knew all about being chased to exhaustion so she took pity on Furry, quickly dragging her to the safety of her den.

When Furry came around from her deep sleep, she was well shocked by the presence of the sly fox. Sunlight reassured the shaking squirrel that she had no intentions of harming her, with the two quickly becoming friends. Furry told Sunlight all about what had happened – in literally falling on the sympathetic fox's doorstep.

Upon hearing the story, Sunlight pledged to do all she could to help her. The wily beast made up a cunning plan; her friend Thorn Owl would deliver a message to Barkeye, informing him that she had Furry hostage and would give her to him for a brace of pheasants.

Barkeye quickly received the message, but, as always, the suspicious leader decided to take his entire army, in case of a trap. Furry, having had such a restful night in Sunlight's company, was now a little anxious as to the day's events.

The morning was fresh and dressed in beautiful sunshine as they waited for Barkeye.

They didn't wait long, Barkeye and his grey army arrived outside the deceitful fox's den.

Both Sunlight and Furry were inside. "Now I want you to do everything I say, little one," said the courageous fox.

Chapter Eight

Sunlight explained to Furry; "I am going outside and you must not make a sound or follow me. Everything will be ok, as long as you stay hidden here, just trust me."

Sunlight moved outside to face the evil grey leader. "Well you didn't think I would hold her here, did you?" she convincingly suggested. Laughing she went on, "So you could come here, just kill me and take the red away? No way, Farteye."

"My name's Barkeye!" he raged. "Where is she? You will get your brace of pheasant if you hand her over."

"Ok, follow me."

Furry drew a sigh of relief as they all could be heard venturing off into the distance. She did as she was asked by staying put, but she started wondering about her destiny. Would the greys eventually wipe them all out?

Sunlight led the army deep into the heart of the forest. "How much further, foxy?" Barkeye asked curiously.

"Not much further now," she replied, having decided it was time to make a break for freedom.

Sunlight's ears pricked; she could hear noises on the horizon, getting closer all the time. This was her best chance.

Sunlight tore away from the army of greys and ran for her life towards the distinctive sounds coming from ahead.

"I knew it!" Barkeye shouted in dismay. "Never trust a fox!"

In haste, he led his army in chase of her. Lord Grief and his gentry stood in the clearing a hundred yards on.

Chapter Nine

His lordship, head of the pheasant hunters, was stood armed, waiting for the arrival of his friends in the forest.

"Beautiful day Giles," he said to his colleague, who turned and agreed.

"Yes my Lord. Ah! Here they come!"

Sunlight caught sight of men on horseback appear in the forest. Their guns fired noisily as they spotted their game running from in the bushes.

Sunlight could feel the ground vibrating from all the galloping paws.

Suddenly she collapsed into the long grass - a stray bullet had struck her head!

Within seconds, Barkeye and the army swarmed on her like vultures to kill her off.

"I say Giles, what the hell is going on over there?" Lord Grief cried out. "Grey squirrels, my Lord, they look as though they are after a fox!"

Before he had time to say anything else, even more game were flying out of the bracken just ahead of the ill-fated fox.

"Shoot!" one of the gunmen called out.

Barkeye fell dead to the ground along with several others around him. The rest of the army ran for their lives.

"Ruddy good show Giles, we picked up a bonus there with a fox!"

"Shame about the squirrels, they don't normally come this far out of the woods."

Chapter Ten

Although they didn't get there in time to save Sunlight, Slugger's reds had seen all they needed to see from a short distance behind, being just too late to help.

They knew of Sunlight's plan to sacrifice herself in the hope of ensuring Furry's freedom. Her loyal friend Thorn Owl had returned and told the reds her intentions. They stood in silence over her lifeless body, in disbelief of having witnessed the terrible price she had paid for all her bravery.

The squirrels returned back to their home, with the news that Sunlight had laid down her life for all of them so they could live in peace and harmony once more. Slugger in her memory, carved out her name on the trunk of a young tree in Bluebell Branches, where the sun always shone the longest.

Angel had miraculously survived from her wounds along with several others, and Furry seemed no worse off from her dangerous encounter.

Things gradually returned back to normal in Bright Side, with the red squirrels happily enjoying day to day life in the neighbourhood once more.

A year on and there has not been a sign of one grey, at least up until now…